SOME SWAHILI WORDS

Chumvi
salt

Jambo
hello

Kula
eat

Kwaheri
good-bye

Ni
I am

THE
LION KING

NALA'S DARE

by Joanne Barkan

Illustrations by Laureen Burger
Brooks & Rachelle Campbell
Denise Shimabukuro

Produced by Mega-Books, Inc. Design and art direction by Michaelis/Carpelis Design Assoc., Inc.
Printed in the United States of America.

Grolier Books

ISBN: 0-7172-8347-X

CHAPTER 1

"When I'm the Lion King," Kopa said, "I'll roar so loud the umbrella thorn trees will drop their leaves!"

Kopa scampered through the trees behind his monkey friends Jambo and Kwaheri.

"I'll be the bravest of the brave!" Kopa shouted. He looked at Jambo and Kwaheri to make sure they were listening to him.

Kerflump! Kopa tripped over a branch and fell to the ground.

Jambo and Kwaheri burst out laughing.

"What a gas! What a goof! What a riot!" said Jambo.

"Tickles my ribs, splits my sides, flips my wig!" Kwaheri said. "Can you believe he's going to be the Lion King someday?"

"Like his father, Simba!" said Jambo. "That's a scream, a hoot, and a howler!"

"Okay, okay," said Kopa. He shook the grass off his back. "Why don't the two of you just drop it?"

"Hey, catch this," said Jambo. "Let's play I-dare-you."

"Cool, fab, outta sight!" said Kwaheri.

"You can say that again!" said Kopa.

"Sure can," said Kwaheri. "Cool—"

"Give it a rest," said Kopa. "I've got the first dare. I dare Jambo to swing from that short acacia tree to that tall one."

"*Hakuna matata*, no problem, no big deal," Jambo said. He scrambled over the grass and climbed the tree. Dangling from a branch with one long arm, he swung back and forth. When he was swinging high enough, he let go of the branch, flew through the air, and grabbed a limb of the taller tree.

"All right! Way to go! Right on!" said Kwaheri. "Now I've got a dare for Kopa. See that pointed rock over there? I dare you to jump off it."

"Just watch me!" said Kopa.

He dashed to the rock and clambered up. From the top, the ground seemed far away. But it was covered with grass.

"Look out below!" Kopa yelled as he jumped.

He landed on all fours and heard Jambo and Kwaheri cheering behind him. Then he heard the flapping of wings.

"Aw, phooey!" he muttered, looking up. "It's the flying pest!"

"I beg your pardon," said the hornbill, hovering above him. "What did you say?"

Kopa sighed. "Nothing, Zazu."

Zazu fluttered to the ground and carefully arranged his feathers. "I should hope not, my young friend. I am your father's trusted steward. I have some responsibility for your welfare."

Kopa sighed again. "I know."

"Well," said Zazu, "I'm on my way back to Pride Rock to deliver a report to your father. A most interesting report. The leopards will be sending us two ambassadors this year instead of one."

Kopa tried to hide a yawn behind a furry paw.

"Ahem—well, I don't suppose that interests you yet," Zazu went on. "The reason I've stopped by is to warn you about the gorge. You mustn't get any closer to it. The water is high after yesterday's rain. And the rocks are slippery. Do you understand?"

"Yes, Zazu," said Kopa. He twitched his tail impatiently.

Zazu glanced at the sun. "Almost two o'clock!" he gasped. "I must be off."

As soon as he had flown away, Jambo and Kwaheri ran up to Kopa.

"Listen up, zero in, and get this!" said

Jambo. "We both dare you to catch us!"

"You're on!" said Kopa.

"Hello!" said Jambo.

"Good-bye!" said Kwaheri.

They bounded away over the uneven ground. Kopa ran as fast as he could, but he couldn't catch them. He lowered his head and concentrated on running faster.

The grass gave way to rocks, but Kopa kept running. Then the rocks became wet and slick. Kopa's claws couldn't grip them. He skidded. His front paws stopped at the edge of the gorge.

"Yikes!" Kopa squealed. He peered over the edge. The narrow stream had become a churning torrent, swollen by rain. It swirled around jagged boulders.

"Kopa, heads up! Get a load of this! Clap your eyes on us!" called Kwaheri.

Kopa looked up. The monkeys were swinging from branches that hung over the torrent. Then *whoosh!* They flew through the air and landed in a tree on the other side of the gorge.

"Hurry up and catch us!" Jambo shouted at Kopa. "Shake a leg! Move it! Get cracking!"

"I can't swing from trees like you," Kopa yelled back.

"Then jump across the gorge!" shouted Kwaheri. "It's not too wide."

Kopa stared at the gorge. It looked wide to him. Maybe I could make it across, he thought. But maybe not. He didn't move.

"Hey, what are you waiting for?" Jambo shouted. "We dare you!"

"Lily liver, yellow belly, jelly paws!" yelled Kwaheri. "You're no Lion King!"

Kopa's heart pounded. His ears were ringing. I shouldn't try it, he thought. It's too dangerous.

The monkeys kept chanting. "Scaredy-cat! Scaredy-cat! Scaredy-cat!"

The noise of rushing water and shouting roared inside Kopa's head. He took a deep breath. He bent his knees.

He screamed, "I'm going to jump!"

CHAPTER

2

Kopa froze. He remained crouched
on the edge of the gorge with his
eyes shut.

"Kitty-cat! Fraidycat! Scaredy-cat!"
Jambo and Kwaheri chanted.

Kopa turned and ran as fast as he
could. He paid no attention to where he
was going. He ran through the trees and
into the tall grass of the open plain.
When the roaring in his head finally
stopped, he slowed down. He gasped for
breath. His gasps turned into sobs.

Maybe I *am* a scaredy-cat, he thought.

Kopa stumbled along until he came to
a deep burrow. Without thinking, he

crawled inside and sat huddled in the darkness, shaking. He sat for a long time.

Clackety-clack. Clackety-clack.

Kopa's ears twitched. "What was that?" he muttered. "There's something outside! A vulture! A wild dog!" He shivered. Then he scowled. "Why am I afraid of a dumb noise?"

Kopa jumped up and scrambled out of the burrow. He stood in the high grass and shouted as loud as he could. "Whatever you are—I'm not afraid of you! Not one bit!"

"Maybe you should be," said a quiet voice.

The grasses parted, and an ancient baboon stood before Kopa. His back was bent, and he leaned on a tall stick. Two gourds were tied to the stick near its top. They knocked against each other. *Clackety-clack.*

"Rafiki!" Kopa cried.

"So I am," said the baboon.

"But how did you find me?" Kopa

asked. "I was hiding. And you haven't come around Pride Rock since we celebrated the rains."

Rafiki shrugged. "What makes you think I was looking for you? Why should I bother with a cub who's foolish enough to crawl into a hyena's den?"

Kopa gasped. "Hyena's den!" Then he tossed his head. "I'm not afraid of hyenas."

Rafiki sighed. "Brave animals know when to be afraid."

"Well, I don't want to be afraid ever!" said Kopa. "I want to jump across gorges and take every dare. I want to be brave all the time like my father and mother!"

Rafiki chuckled. "You think Simba and Nala have never been afraid?"

Kopa thrust out his chin. "Never!"

Rafiki bent down until his head was close to the cub's. He whispered in Kopa's ear, "Ask your mother to tell you the story of Ni."

"What's that?" Kopa asked.

"The story of Ni." Rafiki chuckled. Nodding, he took a few steps back—and disappeared into the tall grass.

Kopa stared at the grass. Then he turned toward Pride Rock. Its massive stones were silhouetted against the deep blue sky.

What's he talking about? Kopa wondered. Dad and Mom afraid? Could it be true? I've got to hear that story!

Kopa raced back to Pride Rock and barreled up to the ledge where he and his parents slept. Simba and Nala were napping.

"Dad! Mom!" Kopa called.

Nala slowly raised her head. When she saw Kopa, she sat up.

"What happened to you?" she asked. "You're covered with dirt. And you've been crying." She pulled Kopa close to her and nuzzled his face.

Simba rolled over and studied his son. "Are you all right?" Simba asked.

Kopa wriggled impatiently. "I'm fine.

Really I am. But there's a story I want to hear. Mom, tell me the story of Ni."

"The story of Ni!" Nala said. "How in the world did you find out about that?"

"From Rafiki," said Kopa. "Come on, Mom. He said you should tell me the story."

"Rafiki," said Nala. "I see . . ." Her large golden eyes sparkled.

Simba pretended to frown. "What story is this?" he asked. "Why don't I know it?"

"Yeah, why doesn't Dad know it?" Kopa asked.

"Because," Nala said, "it happened during the terrible time when Scar was the Lion King. Your father was living in a faraway jungle."

Simba nodded. "I've told you a little about that time, Kopa," he said. "My own father was killed. I ran away because I thought it was my fault. But my father had been killed by my uncle, his evil brother, Scar, who wanted to be king."

"I found your father in that faraway jungle living with his friends Timon and Pumbaa," said Nala. "I asked him to take his rightful place as king. He returned to Pride Rock, fought Scar, and won."

"But the story of Ni happened before you found Dad in the jungle," said Kopa. "Right?"

"That's right," said Nala.

"So where were you living?" Kopa asked his mother. "On Pride Rock? How old were you? Were you as big as me?"

"I was a little older than you," Nala said. She tapped Kopa on the nose with her paw. "I was old enough to know how to listen!"

"Okay," said Kopa. "I'll be quiet. I promise. Please tell us the story."

Simba settled himself into a comfortable position. Kopa snuggled between his father's front legs.

"Yes, tell us," Simba said.

So Nala began the story of Ni.

CHAPTER

S ee you later, Mom," Nala called.
She trotted past a group of
lionesses gathered on a wide rock
terrace. The sun was low in the sky. One
of the lionesses, Sarafina, stood up.

"Where are you off to, dear?" she
asked.

Nala stopped. "To the ledge," she said
to her mother. "With Kula and Chumvi."

Kula and Chumvi were Nala's best
friends.

Sarafina looked worried. "Don't
leave Pride Rock," she said. "There are
hyenas all over the Pride Lands now. It's
dangerous."

"I know, I know," Nala said with a sigh. "Nothing's the way it used to be now that Scar's the Lion King."

Nala crossed the terrace and found her friends waiting.

"Better late than never," said Chumvi. He jumped up and shook himself. "Let's move!"

Kula stretched. "Maybe we should have a snack first," she said.

Nala laughed. "You have food on the brain—all the time!"

"I'm still a growing girl," Kula said. "And dinners have been pretty skimpy lately."

Nala nodded. "Ever since Scar let the hyenas hunt on the Pride Lands."

The three friends headed for their favorite spot—a long ledge on the far side of Pride Rock. It overlooked the parched grasslands and the distant mountains. It was almost always deserted.

"You know," Chumvi said as they walked along, "I was just thinking—"

"Thinking?" said Nala. "Reeeeally?"

Chumvi swatted Nala with his tail. "I was thinking that lions are by far the best animals around. We are superior beings." He raised his head high and pointed his chin up.

Nala shrugged. "Other animals are just different from us."

"No kidding!" Chumvi said. "Like anteaters." He lowered his head to the ground and poked around with his nose.

Kula laughed. "Did you find some bugs?"

"And what about the giraffe?" Chumvi asked. He stretched his neck up as far as he could. "Pretty dumb-looking!"

Kula stretched her neck too.

"Listen, pea-brains," said Nala. "Because they have long necks, giraffes can reach leaves that other animals can't."

"Hippos!" said Kula. "What total goofs!" She spread her legs far apart and lumbered along the trail.

Chumvi imitated her. He threw his

head back and opened his mouth as wide as he could.

"Gross!" he said, laughing. "And elephants are just as ridiculous."

He held a front leg in front of his face and waved it back and forth like a trunk. Kula did the same thing.

"Sorry, guys," said Nala. "I think elephants get the last laugh. They're so big that even lions don't attack them."

"Lions are still the best animals," said Chumvi. "And I'll tell you something else—"

"Gee, I can't wait to hear," said Nala.

Chumvi went on. "The lions in our pride are better than all the other lions!"

They got to the ledge. Nala sat down with her back to the edge and looked at Chumvi, shaking her head.

"I bet lions from other prides are pretty much like us," she said.

"Would you be brave enough to talk to a strange lion and find out?" asked Chumvi.

"Sure I would," said Nala.

"You wouldn't be afraid?" Kula asked.

"I'm not afraid of anything!" Nala said. "So why would I be afraid of talking to a lion from another pride?"

"I don't believe you," said Chumvi. "I dare you!"

"Fine with me," Nala said. She hated to refuse a dare. And this one sounded easy. She would never meet a strange lion. Other prides never roamed the Pride Lands.

"Okay, then," said Chumvi. "I dare you to talk to that lion over there!"

Nala turned to look down from the ledge. A young lion—a stranger—was lurking in the tall grass at the base of Pride Rock.

"Don't do it," said Kula. "That cat looks kinda weird."

Nala stared at the stranger. His coat was scruffy. His face was dirty. Nala gulped.

"I dare you," Chumvi repeated.

"No sweat," Nala said. Her heart was beating fast. "Here I go."

"Nala, don't!" said Kula. "Let's do something that's fun. Let's go home and get something to eat!"

But Nala started down the cliff. She had taken only a few steps when a mighty roar echoed over Pride Rock.

"R-R-R-R-R-R!" It was followed immediately by a second and a third roar.

Nala stopped in her tracks.

"Come back!" Chumvi shouted to her. "You know what that roaring means!"

"We've got to get home!" Kula yelled. "There's an emergency!"

CHAPTER

ala leaped back up to the ledge.
The three friends looked at one
another, worried.

"Let's go!" said Nala.

They ran down the familiar path to the
other side of Pride Rock.

"Do you think someone's been hurt?"
Chumvi asked.

"Maybe there was a hunting accident,"
said Kula.

"I know one thing," said Nala. "It
must be pretty serious."

Kula groaned. "I hate emergencies.
They ruin my appetite!"

About halfway back, the path veered

around a huge boulder. As the young lions drew near it, they heard a large animal running in their direction. They stopped short, huddled together, and waited.

A lioness bounded around the rock.

"Mom!" Nala shouted.

"There you are!" called Sarafina. "I was so worried about all of you."

"What's going on?" Nala asked.

Sarafina was panting from her run. "An outsider—a lion—was spotted in the Pride Lands. He could be a dangerous rogue. The adults on Pride Rock roared to chase him away."

"We saw him," Kula said.

Sarafina nodded. "He was on the far side of Pride Rock. That's why I was so worried."

"Is he gone?" Chumvi asked.

"We're not sure," Sarafina said. "And even if he is, he might return."

Sarafina bustled the young lions back to the rock terrace. Then she went to

speak with the other adults.

Chumvi nudged Nala and laughed. "You are one lucky lion," he said.

"Why?" Nala asked.

"You got out of that dare," said Chumvi. "I knew you wouldn't go near that creepy lion! No one in the world is that brave!"

"Hey! What do you mean?" Nala cried. "I can be that brave!" She looked down and batted a tuft of grass with her paw.

And maybe I can be even braver, she thought. Maybe someday I'll be brave enough to do something about Scar!

Before Nala had a chance to say more, Chumvi said, "I've got to go. My mom won't let me stay out late anymore."

"See you tomorrow," said Kula.

As soon as Chumvi dashed off, Nala said, "He's in for a big surprise. I'm not dropping the dare. Only cowards do that."

"Come on, Nala," said Kula. "Don't

be a lunatic. Maybe you're thinking crazy things because you're hungry. Yeah, maybe you're light-headed from hunger."

"I told you—I'm not afraid of anything," Nala insisted. "And I don't get out of dares. Chumvi thinks I'm chicken, but I'm not."

"Nala, get real," said Kula. "That strange lion could be superdangerous."

Nala stared straight ahead. "I'll get up before dawn—before my mom gets up. And I'll look for that lion on the far side of Pride Rock."

"You're nuts, crazed, psycho, unhinged!" said Kula. "Do you hear me?" She sighed. "Well, I guess I'll have to get up before dawn and stop you."

"No, you won't," said Nala. "It's a dare, and I'm not backing down."

"But you're my friend," said Kula.

Nala nudged Kula's neck gently with the top of her head. "Thanks," she said. "But I've got to show myself what I can do." Then she added with a laugh, "And if I know you, you'll sleep through the morning. You've never gotten up before dawn in your life!"

Much later that night, Nala lay next to her mother on the ledge. She listened to Sarafina's quiet breathing. Nala's eyes were wide open. Every time she thought of the strange, rough-looking lion, she shivered and felt her heart beat faster.

I wish I could fall asleep and not get up for a week! she thought. Then that stupid lion would be gone. And so would this stupid dare.

Another hour dragged by. Finally, Nala fell into a deep sleep.

A strange orange light enveloped the plain. Nala stood beneath an outcropping of rock. A large animal appeared at the top of the rock. It was an anteater.

"Who are you?" Nala called out.

The anteater didn't answer. But as Nala watched, its neck grew longer and longer. Large brown patches appeared on its body.

Nala gasped. "It's turning into a giraffe!"

The giraffe yawned. Its open mouth grew bigger and bigger. Its legs became short and thick. Its body swelled and turned gray.

"Now it's a hippopotamus!" said Nala.

The hippopotamus's nose stretched into a long hose. Its ears turned into huge flaps. Its legs became longer.

"An elephant!" Nala cried.

The elephant sank down on its knees and growled.

"Hey, elephants don't growl," said Nala.

But the elephant wasn't an elephant anymore. It was a crouched lion. A scruffy, dirty lion.

"Hello! Hello!" Nala shouted.

The lion snarled and extended its claws. It leaped off the rock. It leaped right at Nala!

CHAPTER

ala sprang up. The cave was still dark. Sarafina was sleeping quietly.

"What a nightmare!" muttered Nala.

She shook her head, as if to shake the dream out of it. She stretched her legs and crept out onto the ledge. The sky had started to lighten.

Nala headed for the path.

"Psssst!"

Nala's head snapped around. Kula was waiting in the shadow of a rock.

"You got up!" Nala whispered.

"Don't do this, Nala," said Kula. "It's too dangerous."

Nala shrugged impatiently.

"Well, at least have something to eat before you throw yourself at that lion," said Kula.

"Do you have some food?" Nala asked. Her stomach growled.

"I have a little stash," said Kula. "Saved from dinner last night. Come on!"

Nala followed Kula through a narrow passage between two rocks.

"Here's my secret hiding place," Kula whispered. She pushed aside a pile of twigs and leaves, uncovering a deep hole.

Nala peered inside.

"It's empty," she said.

"What?" cried Kula. She looked inside. "Howling hippos! I've been robbed! Someone took my food!"

"Who could have done it?" asked Nala.

"I'll tell you who," said Kula. "It was that creepo lion, that lousy, dangerous prowler you want to make friends with!"

"You don't know that," Nala said.

"Yeah, well, that's who I think it was," said Kula. "And I'm going back to the terrace to tell everyone."

"No!" said Nala. "At least wait until I have a chance to find him. Come on, Kula. I can't drop this dare. I've got to show Chumvi—and myself!"

Kula glared at Nala but didn't say anything. She followed Nala all the way to the far side of Pride Rock.

When they got to the ledge, Nala said, "Wait for me right here."

"Don't do it!" Kula pleaded again.

Nala looked up at the sky and let out a long breath. "Okay, let's make a deal. If I'm not back in ten minutes, then you can start worrying. Until then, relax."

"Gee, some deal," muttered Kula. "Thanks a lot." But when Nala started down the cliff, Kula let her go.

As Nala climbed down, she whispered to herself, "One step at a time. I am not going to be afraid." She watched her footing on the loose rocks.

When she got to the bottom, Nala took a deep breath and plunged into the tall, dry grass. With every step, her heart beat faster and faster.

"He could be anywhere," she murmured. "He could be stalking me right now!"

Nala was afraid—and she knew it.

She walked on, sniffing and looking from side to side. The air was chilly, but she felt warm.

"What's that smell?" Nala whispered. She stopped and sniffed again. "Food."

She lowered her head and pushed through the grass toward the smell. She came to a small burrow and crouched to examine it.

"That's food from last night's dinner," Nala said. "It must be Kula's stash!"

The grass behind her rustled. Nala jerked up her head. Her nostrils flared. Without even looking around, she sprang forward and began to run for her life. She tore through brambles and jumped over stones. And all the while, something raced at her heels.

Run faster! a voice screamed inside her head. Run faster!

Nala pushed through the last of the tall grass. She found herself running on open ground. An outcropping of rock lay straight ahead. She raced toward it. The sounds of running pounded in her head. The footsteps behind her closed in.

Nala strained toward the rock. Suddenly the lion stranger—scruffy and dirty—appeared at the top of the rock. He crouched and extended his claws.

Nala gasped. "It's my nightmare come true!"

The lion snarled at Nala—and sprang!

CHAPTER

N ala braced herself for the crash.
But the lion sailed past her. Nala
whirled.

"A-HEE-EE-EE-EE!" A great buff-
colored hyena screeched and lunged for
Nala. His bone-crunching jaws were
open. His razor-sharp teeth were bared.

"No!" Nala screamed.

The strange lion slammed into the
hyena and sent him flying. The hyena
screeched again and landed on his back.

The lion tumbled once and
jumped up. "Run!" he roared at Nala.
He streaked past her and roared
again, "Run!"

Nala charged after the stranger. His flying feet kicked up loose dirt and pebbles. Nala's shorter legs couldn't keep up. She fell behind. The stranger seemed to sense this. He slowed his pace and turned around.

"Hurry!" he shouted. "That hyena only had the wind knocked out of him. You don't want to be out here alone."

Nala caught up with the lion, and they ran together to an acacia tree. The stranger climbed the tree and slithered onto a sturdy branch. Nala followed him. They scanned the plain for a sign of the hyena. He was nowhere to be seen.

For a few minutes, Nala and the lion didn't speak. They were both recovering from the run.

Finally Nala said, "I thought you were going to attack me. But instead you saved my life."

"I don't attack other lions," said the stranger. "And especially not young flaky ones like you."

"I'm not flaky," Nala snapped.

"Then what were you doing prowling around the plain alone?" asked the stranger. "You know you're still too small to protect yourself."

Nala shrugged. "Oh, it was sort of a dare."

"See, I was right," said the stranger. "You are flaky."

Nala changed the subject. "Who are you, anyway? What's your name?" Then she added, "I'm Nala."

"I'm Ni," the stranger replied.

"What are you doing on the Pride Lands?" Nala asked. "Why aren't you with your own pride?"

"I had to leave," Ni said. "All young males leave their prides when they can survive on their own. You should know that."

Nala nodded. "I guess I thought you were younger," she said. Then she turned away in embarrassment. "Oops. Maybe that was a dumb thing to say."

Ni laughed. "It's true I'm a little smaller than average. It just means I can't afford to be flaky."

"Do you want to come to Pride Rock with me?" Nala asked. "You can meet my two best friends and my mom."

"I don't think I'd be very welcome," Ni answered. "Your pride tried to scare me away yesterday."

"Yeah, but today you're a hero!" said Nala. "You saved my life. When I tell everyone that, they'll like you."

"I'm not so sure," said Ni.

"Well, I am," said Nala. "Come on. Please?"

"Okay," Ni finally said. "Lead the way."

Nala and Ni trotted back to Pride Rock. They began climbing up the steep slope to the ledge. The sun was already hot. Ni moved briskly.

"Climbing down was much easier than climbing up," said Nala. She was winded.

"You won't find it so hard once your

legs are a little longer," said Ni.

About three quarters of the way to the top, Nala stopped to catch her breath. Ni was ahead of her. Nala thought she heard a noise somewhere below. She turned to look. There was nothing there.

"Just the breeze," Nala murmured. She began climbing again.

"Ni," Nala called after a minute. "Can you stay until after the hunt tonight? Then we can—"

Nala heard another sound. Again she turned her head. This time, she screamed.

Just below her crouched the big buff-colored hyena. His jaws were open. His eyes glinted.

CHAPTER

7

Ni whirled around. There was a loud rustling. Four other hyenas sprang from behind the rocks. Nala was surrounded!

She opened her mouth to scream again. But nothing came out. Ni can't save me! she thought. He can't fight off five of them!

The snarling hyenas moved toward her. Ni bent his legs, ready to jump.

"R-R-R-R-R-R!" The sound of a furious roar exploded over the cliff. The rocks seemed to shudder from the force of it.

Sarafina sprang into view. Her

muscular body loomed over the top of the ledge. Kula and Chumvi were just behind her.

Ni and Sarafina leaped through the air in the same instant. Their growling voices merged into one sound. The hyenas cowered. The two lions landed between the hyenas and Nala. The hyenas spun around to flee. They scrambled down the side of the cliff.

Sarafina jumped down a few feet and roared once more. When she'd made sure that the hyenas weren't coming back, she returned.

"Nala, are you hurt?" She licked her daughter's face and shoulders. She checked her back and legs.

"I'm okay," Nala said. But she was trembling. She didn't try to pull away from Sarafina's licking as she sometimes did.

Sarafina stood back and said, "Kula came for me. Luckily she has a head on her shoulders." Sarafina sighed. "You

were very foolish to go out on the plain by yourself."

Nala hung her head. "I know," she said. "I won't do it again." She looked up. "Ni saved my life out on the plain too. That big hyena charged me. Ni chased him away."

Sarafina turned to the scruffy young lion. She studied him for a moment.

"Thank you for what you did," said Sarafina. "It's lucky for our pride that you didn't leave yesterday. I'm sorry that we tried to scare you off, but—"

"It's your right to protect your lands," Ni said. "I understand that."

"Then I hope you'll come back with us now," Sarafina said. "I'd like to introduce you to the others. I want them to know what you've done."

Nala rubbed up against her mother. "Thanks, Mom," she whispered. Then she said to Ni, "Please come."

"I will," said Ni.

They climbed up to the ledge. Chumvi

and Kula were waiting for them. Sarafina led the way back to the other side of Pride Rock. Ni followed her. The three young lions brought up the rear.

"Nala," said Chumvi, "I'm sorry I teased you. It was a crummy thing to do to a friend. I was so worried about you!"

Chumvi and Nala rubbed shoulders. Then, laughing, they tried to jostle each other off the path.

"Hey, did that guy Ni really save you?" Kula asked.

"Yup," said Nala. "The hyena was about to pounce on me. Ni jumped off a huge rock and knocked him over."

"Wow!" said Chumvi. "Weren't you scared?"

Nala hesitated for a second and then answered with a little cough. "Yes."

"You know," whispered Kula, "if Ni washed and groomed his fur, he'd be sort of . . . cute."

Nala glanced at Ni and whispered in Kula's ear, "I think so too."

When they got back to the terrace, Sarafina introduced Ni to everyone. By the time the story was told and questions had been answered, the sun was high.

The adults spent the afternoon resting in the shade. Nala and her friends shared a snack with Ni. Then they showed him the best trees for climbing and their favorite caves. They had wrestling matches and played stalk-and-ambush.

When the sun was low in the sky, Ni said, "It's time for me to go."

"Not yet!" Nala protested.

Ni nodded.

"But you can't leave without seeing the summit of Pride Rock," Nala said.

"Okay, show me the summit," said Ni. "But then I'll have to leave."

Ni said good-bye to Kula and Chumvi. Then he and Nala took a winding path up to the summit. They stood on a high, flat rock and gazed down at the plain.

The dry grass reflected the last of the golden light. A few antelopes and a zebra were still grazing. Beyond the plain rose a plateau in purple shadow. And beyond the plateau stood the deep blue peaks of the mountains.

"I can remember when it looked very different here," said Nala. "There used to be so many wildebeests and zebras and gazelles, you couldn't even count them."

"Maybe someday you'll help to change it back to the way it was," Ni said.

"Maybe," said Nala. She was silent for a minute. Then she asked, "Where are you going? Will you always be alone? Will you ever have a pride?"

Ni laughed and shrugged. "Who knows? Maybe I'll grow strong enough to win a pride from another lion. Maybe not."

"You're brave enough to do it!" Nala said. "I want to be brave too. I don't want to be afraid of anything!"

"Even dangerous dares?" asked Ni.

"But if you don't take a dare, then everyone says that you're afraid," Nala argued. "And maybe you'll start believing what they say."

Ni stared at her. "You're listening to the monkeys," he said.

"What?" Nala asked.

"Lions who listen to the chattering of monkeys will never learn to roar," Ni chuckled and added, "A wise old baboon once told me that—and he was right."

"I don't get it," said Nala. "I—"

"Sh-sh-sh," said Ni. "Just think about it." He bent his head down and rubbed his cheek gently against Nala's cheek. "Good-bye, my flaky little friend."

"I am not flaky!" said Nala.

But before the words were out of her mouth, Ni had started down a steep path. Nala watched him go. Her eyes followed the tawny color of his fur as he passed between rocks and trees. Down. Down. Down. The sun slipped below the horizon, and Ni disappeared.

"Good-bye," Nala whispered.

CHAPTER

nd then what happened? Did you ever see Ni again, Mom?"

Kopa sat up and nudged Nala with his forehead. She shook herself as if she were coming out of a dream.

"No, I never saw him again," Nala said. She looked at Kopa and Simba. Her eyes filled with love. "But when I was young, I often thought about what he taught me. And now you both know the story of Ni. I'm happy about that."

Simba rose and rubbed his cheek against Nala. "It was a wonderful story."

"But I want to know more," said Kopa. "Did Ni find a pride to live with?

Do you think he'll ever show up around here again?"

Nala and Simba laughed. "Who knows?" they said.

There was a fluttering of wings and then a light tapping on the ledge nearby.

"Three guesses who that is," muttered Kopa. "Aren't we the lucky ones!"

"Please, Kopa," said Simba. "A little respect!"

"Sire? May I see you?"

"Of course, Zazu," said Simba.

Zazu hopped over to them and stood before Simba. He puffed out his chest and held his tail feathers straight up. He nodded politely to Nala and Kopa.

"I have the afternoon report, sire," he said. "Would you like to hear it now? Or shall I come back later? I don't like to interrupt young Kopa's quality time with his parents."

Kopa made a gagging noise. Simba gave him a gentle swat with his tail.

"Now is fine," said Simba.

"Good, sire," said Zazu. "I have some particularly interesting statistics on the rate of leaf production for year-old umbrella thorn trees. If you factor in the average rainfall since—"

"I'm going to suffocate," Kopa said under his breath. "I'm going to keel over and—"

"Kopa," said Nala, "if you'd like to go and play, just ask politely."

"May I?" Kopa asked. "Please?"

Nala nodded.

Zazu gave a little laugh. "Oh, cubs will be cubs!" Then he added, "Ah, yes! That reminds me—I saw your friends, those monkeys, just a few minutes ago. They were looking for you. They said they'd be around the terrace."

"Thanks, Zazu," Kopa said, and he ambled across the terrace, waving his tail back and forth. He hummed a song and thought about the story of Ni.

"Yo, Kopa! Howdy-do! What's happening, baby? How's tricks?"

Kopa's eyes followed the sounds. He saw Jambo and Kwaheri dangling from the branches of an umbrella thorn tree. Kopa scampered toward them.

"Watch this, Kopa!" shouted Jambo. Holding a branch with one hand, he swung higher and higher. Then he let go of the branch, did a double somersault in the air, and landed just in front of Kopa.

"Hey, catch this!" shouted Kwaheri. He held onto a branch with his tail and swung higher and higher. Then he flew through the air, did a triple somersault, and landed just in back of Kopa.

"Your turn! Up you go! Show your stuff!" said Jambo.

"Yeah, what are you waiting for? The clock's ticking. Time's a-wasting," said Kwaheri.

"You know I can't do those things," Kopa said. "Stop bugging me about it."

"I dare you!" said Jambo. "You're not a scaredy-cat, are you?"

Kopa tossed his head and started to walk away.

"Hey, where are you going? What's the deal? What's up?" asked Kwaheri.

Kopa turned and looked at his friends. He puffed out his chest and held his head high. He said, "Lions who listen to the chattering of monkeys will never learn to roar!"

Jambo and Kwaheri stared at Kopa. Their mouths opened. "Huh?"

Kopa listened to their unusual silence. He liked it. Then he heard a faint noise. *Clackety-clack. Clackety-clack.*

Kopa looked all around. He thought he saw a tall stick with two gourds on it in a tree. He rubbed his eyes. When he looked again, it was gone.

But far away, someone was chuckling.